This Book Belongs To

. . . .

A Catalogue record for this book is available from the
British Library

ISBN 0 340 73985 1

Printed and bound in Great Britain by The Devonshire
Press, Torquay, Devon TQ2 7NX

Hodder Children's Books
a division of Hodder Headline plc
338 Euston Road
London NW1 3BH

Little Blue

sings a song

Margaret Ryan

illustrated by Andy Ellis

**Hodder
Children's
Books**

a division of Hodder Headline plc

For Maureen
with love
- M.R.

For Oliver
- A.E.

Little Blue was having
breakfast when
Postman Pen arrived.

"A letter for you, Little Blue,"
he said.
"Oh good," said Little Blue.
"I love getting letters."

He opened the envelope and took out the letter.

"It's a special letter," he said to his mum and dad. "It's an invitation to Rocky's birthday party. Look it says..."

Dear Little Blue,

Please come to
my birthday party this
afternoon.

There will be lots to
eat and drink and
3 special competitions.

1. The biggest beak
   competition.

2. The biggest feet
   competition.

3. The biggest voice
   competition.

The prizes are fish
flavoured ice-creams.

See you soon,

love Rocky.

Little Blue jumped up and
down and waved his
invitation in the air.
"I can't wait to go," he said.
"I love parties. I love
competitions. I love fish-
flavoured ice creams."

"And I love peace and quiet,"
said his dad.

But Little Blue took no notice.
He was thinking about the
competitions.

"The biggest beak competition," he said. "I don't think I could win that. I don't think my beak's big enough yet."
He went over to the mirror to check. His beak didn't LOOK very big.

"Perhaps I could try to stretch it," he said, and he grabbed his beak in his flippers and pulled and pulled.

But it was no good. No matter how hard Little Blue pulled, his beak didn't get any bigger. So he had another think.

"The biggest feet competition," he said. "I don't think I could win that, either. I don't think my feet are big enough yet."

He lifted each of them up to have a look. His feet didn't LOOK very big.

"Perhaps I could try to stretch them," he said.

And he grabbed each foot in his flippers and pulled and pulled.

But it was no good. No matter
how hard Little Blue pulled,
his feet didn't get any bigger.

He sat down and had
another think.

The biggest voice competition," he said. "THAT'S the one I'll enter for. I'm sure I could win that. I'm sure my voice is big enough. I'll practise using it right away!"

And he began to sing.

"I'M A LITTLE PENGUIN BLUE

I LIKE FISH PUT IN A STEW

I LIKE TOAST WITH SARDINES
TOO . . .

I'M A LITTLE PENGUIN BLUE!"

"That noise is making my
head ache, Little Blue," said
his mum.

"That noise is making my beak
ache, Little Blue," said his dad.

"Sorry," said Little Blue. "But
I must keep practising for the
biggest voice competition
or I'll never win a fish-
flavoured ice cream, and
they're my favourite."

14

Little Blue's mum looked at
Little Blue's dad.
Little Blue's dad looked at
Little Blue's mum.
"Time to go fishing," they
both said, and left Little Blue
to practise his song.

"I'M A LITTLE PENGUIN BLUE

I LIKE FISH PUT IN A STEW

I LIKE TOAST WITH SARDINES
TOO . . .

I'M A LITTLE PENGUIN BLUE!"

"That sounds really good,"
said Little Blue. "But I don't
know if it's loud enough. I
think I'll go outside and sing
it. Perhaps it'll sound louder
out there."

Little Blue went out of the
upturned boat where he lived
and wandered down to the
water's edge.

There were lots of penguins
there, sunning themselves on
the rocks.

"Hi guys," said Little Blue. "I'm practising for the biggest voice competition at Rocky's party this afternoon. Want to hear my song?"

"Nope," said the penguins.
But Little Blue sang it anyway.

"I'M A LITTLE PENGUIN BLUE

I LIKE FISH PUT IN A STEW

I LIKE TOAST WITH SARDINES
TOO . . .

I'M A LITTLE PENGUIN BLUE!"

"Well what do you think?" he
asked the other penguins
when he'd finished.
The other penguins all looked
at each other.

"We think it's time to go
fishing," they said, and
jumped into the water.
Quickly.

Little Blue was left on the
shore, singing on his own.
"Funny how all the penguins
wanted to go fishing at once,"
he said. "Oh well, I'll go and
find Joey and sing him my
song."

Joey, the little kangaroo,
was fast asleep in his mother's
pouch when Little Blue
arrived.

"I'll sing my song now,"
said Little Blue.
"That'll wake Joey up."

"I'M A LITTLE PENGUIN BLUE

I LIKE FISH PUT IN A STEW

I LIKE TOAST WITH SARDINES
TOO . . .

I'M A LITTLE PENGUIN BLUE!"

"Who's making that racket?"
said Joey, poking his head out
of his mother's pouch. "I was
having a nice little snooze."

"Hi Joey," said Little Blue.
"It's me. I'm practising for the
biggest voice competition at
Rocky's party this afternoon.
Want to hear my song again?"
"No," said Joey. "Come on,
Mum. We have to go." And
they both hopped away.
Quickly.

"That's funny," said Little
Blue. "Kangaroos don't fish.
Oh well, I'll carry on
practising anyway.
This is a good open space
to sing my loudest."
And he began to sing
his song again.

"I'M A LITTLE PENGUIN BLUE

I LIKE FISH PUT IN A STEW

I LIKE TOAST WITH SARDINES TOO . . .

I'M A LITTLE PENGUIN BLUE!"

Just then there was a noise
like distant thunder and Big
Grey and his mob thundered
up. Big Grey skidded to a halt
in a cloud of dust.

"Do you hear what I hear?"
he said to his mob.
"Sounds like someone's
stepped on a spiny ant eater."

"Or someone's EATEN a spiny
ant eater."
"My aunt once ate a spiny ant
eater. YUK!"

"Quiet – and listen," said
Big Grey. "There's that awful
noise again!"

29

"I'M A LITTLE PENGUIN BLUE

I LIKE FISH PUT IN A STEW

I LIKE TOAST WITH SARDINES
TOO . . .

I'M A LITTLE PENGUIN BLUE!"

"I'm off," said Big Grey. "That
noise is giving me earache."
"Me too!" said his mob,
and they all held their ears
and hopped away.
Quickly.

Little Blue sang and sang till it was time to go to the party.

"I'm SURE to win the biggest voice competition now," he said, "after all that practising."

He took a birthday card and
a box of crab-flavoured
candies for Rocky and
set off for the party.
But when he arrived, there
was hardly anybody there.

"Where IS everyone?" asked
Little Blue.
Rocky shook his head sadly.
"They can't come," he said.
"They all live across the bay
and just look who's
out there."

Little Blue looked out across
the bay and saw two dark
triangular shapes sticking out
of the water.
"Oh no," he said. "It's the
sharks, Fick and Fin!"
"No one can swim across
while THEY'RE there,"
said Rocky.

Little Blue sat down and
had a think.

"I have an idea," he said.

"I'll sing them a song."

"A song?" said Rocky.

"How will that help?"

"Just watch," said Little Blue.

And he sang his song at the

top of his voice.

"I'M A LITTLE PENGUIN BLUE

I LIKE FISH PUT IN A STEW

I LIKE TOAST WITH SARDINES
TOO . . .

I'M A LITTLE PENGUIN BLUE!"

Fick and Fin poked their
heads up out of the water.
"Do you hear what I hear,
Fick?" said Fin.
"I hear something TERRIBLE,
Fin," said Fick.
"Like a spiny ant eater that's
been eaten by a shark!"
"Or a shark that's been eaten
by a spiny ant eater!"

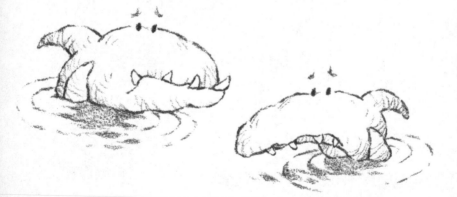

"Don't be silly, Fick," said Fin.
"We're the ones who do the
eating."
"Sorry," said Fick. "It's that
noise! It's making
my brain ache."
"Mine too," said Fin.
"Let's go fishing."
And they swam away.
Quickly.

Rocky was delighted and soon all his friends swam across the bay for the party. They had a great time.

The royal penguin won the biggest beak competition and Joey won the biggest feet competition.

Little Blue won the biggest
voice competition, though
he didn't need to sing
his song again.

"We've heard it already," said
Rocky, who didn't want
everybody to leave the party
to go fishing.

Little Blue went home happy
with three fish-flavoured
ice creams.

"Rocky gave me extra ones
because my singing saved the
party," he told his mum and
dad. "Would you like to hear
my song again?"

"Why don't you eat your ice creams instead," said his mum.

"Good idea!" said Little Blue. "I LOVE fish-flavoured ice creams."

"And I love peace and quiet,"
said his dad.